WAY CROSSER

MIA RAM

Published by Water Dragon Publishing
waterdragonpublishing.com

An imprint of Paper Angel Press
paperangelpress.com

ISBN 978-1-957146-93-5 (Trade Paperback)

10 9 8 7 6 5 4 3 2 1

WAY CROSSER

T HERE IS NOWHERE the sea won't follow.

It was inevitable that Ro, my friend, would sail again. Ro told me, when she came back, that she had truly believed her sailing days were behind her. She'd gotten herself all set up in the university — one of five women in the freshman class of 1872 — living in a box of an apartment by the grounds. She'd said her goodbyes to the captain and the rest of us, and bought her books, her pencil, and a ruler to outline a new life.

It was only three weeks into the semester when she heard them, she said. The waves. They lapped against the glass of the classroom windows. The saltwater licked at her feet beneath the desk, wet her tongue with that sweet, familiar taste. She'd open up the textbook, and the words rose and fell, cresting. When she shut her eyes to sleep, she saw the blue expanse ahead, and a great wave roared in her ears. There could be no denying it. The sea wanted her back.

"I was never still my whole life," she told me when she came back. "And now I don't know how to be."

So, for that fated sail from the Puget Sound port, Ro was amongst us once again, rope in her hands and salt spray tinging her short black hair, like she'd never left us. Our crew had been together long enough to have morphed into something like a family, and Ro was our prodigal daughter come home. Once more we had her bursting smile, the youthful staccato of her running across the ship, her laugh clear like a bell, her unquenchable thirst to go farther, to go faster, always. We loved Ro the way one loved a force of nature, the way one let themselves be drenched in the rain or carried away in the winds.

And I loved her more than any of them, but I was a coward, and so I never said it out loud.

Spirits were high with her return. It was supposed to be an easy trip. We were sailing for Hawaii.

Here's what happened. Believe it if you want.

•　　　•　　　•

It was the first evening of the journey, and we were tossed around like ragdolls. Blackened clouds bubbled above as the ocean roiled in a fury, its behemoth waves rocking the ship — hell, nearly flipping it. It was all we could do to hang on for dear life. I was with the first of the crew to tie ourselves to the mast, before those first drops of rain even fell. I could always sense a bad storm in my bones, almost as well as I can now. Almost as well as I could sense the fear rolling off my shipmates.

Only Ro wasn't afraid. She grew up at sea alongside her sailor parents, raised to love the wildness of storms. The wind and ocean spray blinded me as I prayed to whoever was listening, and all the time I could hear her laughing, which was almost as balming as an actual answer from God might have been. But I prayed through the whole storm nonetheless.

By the time the storm was done with us, we weren't anywhere near Hawaii. We were, as far as we could tell, not anywhere near anywhere.

Ro had a silver compass she'd won at a card game back in Portland. We huddled around her on the deck as she held it in her hand beneath the sun's relentless light. Only the Captain was absent, sleeping off a headache in his quarters.

Jim, a giant of a man, looked over Ro's shoulder. "What's it doing?"

Ro shrugged, furrowing her brows as she gave the compass a petulant shake. "I don't know, the needle just keeps spinning."

"Damn thing's broke," another of the crew, Mary, chimed in.

Ro shook her head. "It was working perfectly before."

"Maybe the storm scrambled it," I suggested, genius that I was. "Got too much water in it, or something."

Ro squinted at the compass as she tapped its side with her finger. Still the needle spun and spun as though it were possessed. We were about to surrender and wake the captain for instructions when, finally, victory lit Ro's face.

"There we go!" She grinned. The needle pointed to her left. She turned her gaze to follow its direction, as we all did.

In the distance loomed an emerald dot. We'd all sailed to Hawaii before, and we knew this island wasn't it.

We argued back and forth about docking. The logical thing was to do so and check the ship for repairs. But something about the look of it, the feel of it, the way it waited, set our teeth on edge. When the Captain emerged, he had us set the sails and turn us off course from the island. But our argument, and the Captain's commands, mattered nothing in the end. No matter which way we turned the sails or shifted the rudder, the waves brought us closer to the island. We struggled hopelessly against the sea as it pulled our ship toward its shore.

•   •   •

Ro was the first one to have her feet hit the sand.

She jogged down the beach before turning toward us, the dark forests blooming behind her. "Shall we treasure hunt?"

"Not on your life," I called back as I disembarked, my eyes not on her, but the wilds close by. She seemed so small against it. Yet wild, too, like she belonged to it.

As the rest of the crew descended, so sprung up the chorus.

"Well, no wonder the rudder wasn't working right, look at this ..."

"Here's a hole as big as my hand ..."

"Old thing's been beaten to hell by the storm ..."

I stood by Ro, listening in on all the assessments by my crewmates as they all added up to an inevitable conclusion: we wouldn't be leaving anytime soon.

"You look like a drowned man," Ro said to me with a smirk, bumping my arm with her elbow.

"What I look like is a man who's not where he's supposed to be," I replied.

"Where's your sense of adventure?"

"Left it in Portland."

"Your sense of discovery?"

"Storm blew it away."

Ro looked at me with pure amazement. "You really aren't excited by any of this, not the slightest bit?"

I shrugged. Excitement was all well and good, but anxiety held its own sacred purpose. Anxiety is the little bell that rings in our heads when something isn't quite right, warning us when we have crossed over into something we shouldn't have. I suspect Ro was born without that little bell.

Ro squeezed my shoulder in a way that made my heart skip. "Breathe in real deep."

I obliged, then paused. Ro grinned.

"What's it smell like?"

"It's like ... like the Cascades." I sucked in another breath, the hesitant statement feeling truer as I did. Yes, yes this was just like the Cascades, the air that raised me.

Ro nodded, then pointed at the forests beyond. "And if you tilt your head, isn't their emerald familiar?"

"I ... I don't know."

"And this shore is downright sparkling. If you told me we've found Eden here, I wouldn't ask twice."

"You read too many books."

Ro shoved me, then called over Mary, Jim, and another fellow named Eddie. As they made their way over, she flashed me another grin.

"They say the greatest fear is that of the unknown. So, let's make this place known."

•   •   •

I've got to tell you, there's nothing like letting yourself be taken in by a strange land. You feel the roots in your feet and the branches in your fingertips. The ocean gets bluer, the trees taller and more twisted, and the world comes secretly alive just for you. What is new makes you new, too.

The rest of the crew were all too happy to let our small group volunteer for a little scouting. I (and likely the other three) only agreed to go to keep Ro from doing something stupid on her own, like leaping down a waterfall or venturing into some underwater cavern. But I'd be lying if I said her giddiness wasn't a little infectious, even when the receding sight of our ship behind us sent my heart racing.

Mary's jaw was perpetually dropped as she surveyed our surroundings. "This doesn't belong to anyone, huh? Pure, untainted land."

"Pure," Jim echoed, nodding. "We ought to name it."

Ro pressed a hand to her chest and dipped her head. "Ro Island, obviously. After the genius navigator who sighted it first."

"Hate to burst your bubble, but there's already a Ro Island," I laughed.

"Well, any island not named 'Hawaii' is pretty much useless to us, isn't it?" Eddie said, looking around with a twitch. "God help us."

"He must have wanted us here, Eddie. Or he wouldn't have steered us to these shores." Ro picked up her pace, leading them farther along the shore.

If we'd have turned back for the ship at that point, I think it would have been alright. Or it would have been different, at least. But Ro always wanted to keep going, farther and farther, always convincing us right when someone suggested we return. And it was hard not to be convinced. The island really could have been Eden. So we went farther and farther, all the way to a wide outcropping of limestone rocks. That's where we saw the other ships.

"Oh my God," Jim said, the rest of us falling to silence as we looked out.

There must have been six washed up there, some on the shore, some crammed between the rocks. Five were large, sailing ships, and one was a rowboat. One ship had been gored through by the rocks, a giant laying with a gaping wound. They all lay battered and desiccated to varying degrees, with torn sails and rotting wood, corpses scattered in a graveyard. The wind blew through them, howling softly like a ghost song.

Ro and the others went down immediately to search for survivors. I dutifully followed behind, but I knew that there would be no living soul below. I was seized by a screaming instinct to turn tail for the ship. Were it not for my pride, I would have. Instead, I swallowed my fear and searched the lost ships with my friends.

"Hello?" Eddie called out, wandering near the biggest ship. "Anybody here?"

Not a sound. We yelled until our throats ached, and only our echoes answered us.

After a while, Ro got me by the shoulder and led me to the least ruined ship that had washed up.

"We need to do a search inside," she said, her voice serious, yet tinged by that unmistakable spark of curiosity. I wanted to board that ship about as much as I wanted to pluck my eye out with a toothpick, but I wasn't about to say no with everyone watching. So we scaled the ropes hanging off the frontside, and got ourselves on the deck. The wood creaked beneath our feet like it was about to snap with every step. Above us, the ivory sails swelled.

"If anyone were down in the cabins, they'd have heard us and come out already, don't you think?" I asked Ro.

Ro shook her head. "Maybe they're injured or knocked out, or … well, you know. Doesn't mean we don't try."

She walked ahead of me, heading for the door that led to the cabins. I steeled myself and followed her down to the shadowed depths of the ship.

It was so dark, I could scarcely see. I had to let the sound of Ro's footsteps lead me. Most frightening tales, this would be the part where I'd say I felt like some other presence was in the ship, watching us. But the terrifying thing was, it was an absence I felt as we scoured the ship. An endlessly deep, barren, absence.

Eventually, we came to a cabin with a window, which was a small comfort. Rays of light peeked through the layers of scum on the glass. It was a nice room, with a bed instead of a cot, a small desk, and a dressing trunk. Not a captain's room, but it had certainly belonged to someone of some importance. Ro looked around, lifting blankets, opening up the desk drawers. All were empty, except for one.

"Now look at this," she muttered, the corner of her mouth turning up faintly. She held in her hands a small book. She flipped through the pages. "Someone left a journal behind."

"That should be illuminating." I checked to see if the trunk was unlocked, searching for more clues.

The lid pulled open with ease. I beckoned Ro over to see. She shut the journal and joined me, and we looked through the contents of the trunk together, trying to piece together this lost story. We looked through clothes, fancy clothes that must have belonged to a man with money. More intriguing than that were his many tools.

Maps, a brass and ivory quadrant, spyglasses and sieves, a contraption of magnifying glasses, flasks and beakers, jars of mysterious powders. There were a few devices I'd never even seen in my life, though Ro seemed to recognize them.

"This is incredible," she whispered, breathless. She looked at me. "We've got to take it back with us."

I frowned. "Isn't that like stealing?"

"You see anyone here to object?" she asked, gesturing at the empty space. She threw the journal into the trunk and closed the lid, then grabbed one end. "Go on, help me haul it up. We can just kind of drop it down on the sand, or lower it with ropes."

Haul it we did, leaving the ship to its eternal silence. The others were waiting below. They were spooked and paler than milk, cowed by the massive shadows cast by the washed-up ships. We all left together, not one of us looking back. Except for Ro.

•   •   •

That night, the crew stayed huddled below deck. Evening had brought more smoke-dark clouds, and we were sure another storm was coming for us. In the distance, thunder screamed and lightning cracked, the waves leaping as though every strike was a whip against the ocean's back. Yet the rains never wet our ship.

"The island's looking out for us," Ro said, lounging on her cot as her eyes grazed the journal's first pages. We who had seen the lost ships were crammed in her quarters.

"I don't know about that," Jim muttered. He was sitting on the floor next to me, whittling a wooden spoon down into a flower with his switchblade. I watched, soothed by the rhythmic strikes of the knife.

Mary, sitting opposite to the recovered trunk, glared at it with suspicion. "Should've guessed from the start this place ain't right. The air hits you different."

"Those damn *rocks* hit you different." Eddie shivered at the memory. "By the grace of God we didn't end up like those poor bastards."

"Those poor bastards wanted to be here." Ro's eyes shot up from the pages. She waved the journal in the air. "They spent years trying to find this island, according to this."

I sat up. "It says that? How long were you sitting on that information?"

"Well, I got caught up in it. It's good reading!"

Jim paused in his whittling. "Well, who were they? And what the hell's this place they wanted to find so badly? Does it have a name?"

Ro shrugged, eyes darting back down to the journal. "He never names the island, exactly. He either calls it 'the island' or sometimes 'the threshold'."

"'He'?" I asked.

"Professor Lawrence Hill. Professor of what, I haven't figured out yet. But he was leading some kind of expedition."

"Maybe he's still leading it," I said, suddenly hopeful. "Maybe that's where they all are, deeper in the island."

Ro nodded to the trunk. "If that's true, why'd he leave his tools?"

I shrugged, my optimism deflating as quickly as it sprung up.

"Let's see these tools." Jim set down his knife and spoon, making for the trunk. He lifted the lid and rifled through the trunk's contents, pausing often to furrow his brow at some contraption or another. As he inspected the brass quadrant, Ro graced us with a look into Professor Lawrence Hill's mind.

Ro read aloud.

> *Cinder and smoke in the air. Monas' texts cite the scent repeatedly as a sign that it's near, along with the blue light. Could it be some alchemical byproduct of crossing over? What transmutation in the fabric of the elements occurs at these crossings, how do we perceive them, and why? I pour over my sources until the oil burns out, and I'm left with more questions than when I began. Tomorrow I will begin studying the* Mary Celeste *crew accounts, which should hopefully be illuminating. Nevertheless, I long to set sail for the island. The threshold. There are others out in the world, I know, but my research leads me to this one again and again. It is a sign. I long to see for myself what the journals and books fail to tell me. With God's help, I will find it.*

"God's help," Jim mumbled to himself, setting the quadrant down and reaching for the maps. "Is that what brought us here?"

Ro traced the words on the page. "He funded everything. The ship, the crew, everything. And he wasn't the first, he says."

"All for this hunk of rock?" I scoffed.

"Maybe. Or maybe something *on* this hunk of rock," said Ro, half to herself. She frowned. "Don't ask me what, Hill was vague. Or maybe I've been skimming too much. Some of the stuff he says goes right over my head. I need to give it a more thorough read."

"Jesus Lord, what kind of maps are these?" Jim squinted down at the yellowed map unfurled in front of him. He beckoned us all to take a look. "C'mere and tell me you see what I see."

We huddled around the map. The top of it was labeled *Pacifica*. On it was the Pacific Ocean, edges crowded with the expected places painted in bleeding watercolor, like the American west coast and Australia. But then there were other landmasses — ones I could tell you for sure didn't exist. Immense islands and continents right in the center of the Pacific. Nonexistent countries and cities were marked within, and with drawings of fantastical creatures, all either labeled with imaginary names or in some unreadable script. Instead of latitude or longitude lines, the map was run through with weaving blue lines that leaped through the landmasses and countries in strange patterns.

"Special kind of map, maybe?" Mary tilted her head as she stared down at it. "I'm not a scientist, I don't know. Ro, you're the *learned* one, what is it?"

Ro took the map in her hands, shaking her head as she poured over it. She brushed her fingers along one of the vast islands. "I don't know. I've never seen anything like this."

Eddie stood up, huffing as though the map were a personal offense to him. "Total nonsense. Your 'Professor Hill' was obviously just a loon, and that's all there is to that mystery. A loon with his own little make-believe map. I've seen and heard enough madness for one night. I'm going to sleep."

We waved him goodbye, lingering to look through the maps a little longer. Soon, Jim and Mary gave up too, leaving us behind for their beds. Exhaustion was catching up to me. Ro, glued to the maps and the journal, was more awake than ever.

I told Ro goodnight, pushing the rest of the maps her way, eager for the refuge of sleep. She nodded, but I don't think she noticed me leave.

•　　•　　•

We set about repairs that next morning. I didn't remember our ship hitting any rocks or anything of the like, but there were jagged holes at the hull. Of course it was strange, but I didn't bother calling it strange, because I was past asking questions. I was just set on doing whatever I needed to do to leave the island and return to normalcy. Plug the holes, one after another.

By midday, I saw Ro talking to the Captain, journal in hand. For a moment, they looked like they were arguing, but after a while he nodded and turned away. She came running towards me then, waving at me.

"Feel like a little adventure?" she asked me.

I was under the bow, holding a cone plug. "After yesterday? Not at all."

"Too bad, because we're going on one." Ro's eyes darted to the vast forest in the distance, hungry. "Captain says we can scout out the woods. Check for survivors of those ships, or signs of them. Just a quick look, not too deep in."

"And if we get lost?" I narrowed my attention back on to the plug, like I could plug Ro's idea same as I could plug a hole on the ship.

"We'll mark the trees as we go."

"Why not take Jim? Or Mary?"

"They already shot me down. Come on, Captain says I've gotta take someone."

I won't lie. As much as I didn't want to go, it stung that she asked me last. Maybe that's what broke down my defenses.

Only for you, Ro. Only for you.

I turned to her with a sigh. "Quick, you said?"

The smile that bloomed on her face when I said that. I'd give my right hand to see it again.

Once more we left the ship behind as I followed Ro into the shivering emerald expanse. The palm trees at the edge leaned forward to invite us in. Ro had her knife. She marked every few trees, slashing in an X and circling it so she'd know it was her mark. As we wandered deeper, sunlight got scarcer, trickling in between the cracks of the canopy.

A jungle is a living thing, you know. I realized that once I was there in its belly. It breathes. It sighs. It whispers to you with the rustling of its leaves and the crunch of twigs beneath your feet. If you let it, it will swallow you whole.

"No sign of human life that I can see," I said after a bit. Ro was staring ahead, knife in one hand, journal gripped in the other.

"But they must be out here, somewhere." Her voice was low, wondering. "Or it must be."

"It?" I repeated, a chill running through me at the way she said it. That glaze in her eyes.

She turned to me and opened the journal. "The thing Professor Hill keeps writing about. He named it here somewhere, hold on ..."

"Well, hold on, what're we looking for, survivors or the professor's tall tales?" I joked, but she was already nose-deep in that journal again — *that damn journal.*

"Here!" Ro's face brightened as she pointed at the word. "'The Way Crosser'. That's what he calls it. Way Crosser. Does that mean anything to you?"

"Why would it?" I snorted. "It sounds meaningless, something your lunatic professor made up."

Ro turned a page. "Way Crosser. Way Crosser. It feels familiar when I say it out loud. Like I've heard it in a dream."

"You remember your dreams?"

"Who doesn't?" She shrugged. She started to read aloud.

Whittle yourself down, says Monas, to the essence. Strip away ego, unravel the things you think of as the threads of yourself, if you seek the Way Crosser, the blue light, the threshold. And Monas certainly unraveled. As the texts go on he begins to ramble and cycle back through the same few incomprehensible phrases. I think I've gotten all the use I can out of his writings. The Mary Celeste *accounts go the same way, descending into babble. This is what comes of a lack of scientific rigor in approaching the unknown. None were ready for contact with the Way Crosser. None were ready to finish what they began, to take the final leap. None were worthy. I intend to be.*

I tried to lighten the mood. "Thought highly of himself, I take it."

Ro closed the journal again, slowly, as though it physically pained her to do so. "He seems like a smart man."

"If he was so smart, we wouldn't be looking for him right now." I looked around, nerves dancing at all the dark corners. "Let's head back."

"What? It's not even been an hour yet!"

"Don't care. I'm working up a fever here." I wiped the beads of sweat off my forehead with my sleeve.

Ro looked out toward the distance again, biting her lip. "You think they're on the other side of the island?" she asked me.

The answer tore its way out of me without a thought. "No."

"They must be here, somewhere. They must be, right?"

"Must be," I muttered, but that was a lie. I couldn't tell you how or why, but we both knew that we could scour this island for a thousand years and never find those sailors.

A breeze blew through the branches, and the jungle laughed.

"Let's go back," Ro finally said, smaller than she'd been when we set out.

She scoped out the last tree she'd marked and led us down the trail, brushing each encircled X with her fingertips as we passed them by. I followed. And followed. And followed.

•　　•　　•

"We're lost."

I tried to say it matter-of-factly, with the kind of authoritative calm the Captain used when it was time to deliver bad news. It came out like a squeak.

Ro bristled. Her face was streaked with dirt and sweat. She pointed at the tree just ahead, scarred with her tell-tale symbol. "We're not lost. I marked this tree. It's on the path. We'll be back at the shore in minutes."

"You said that hours ago."

"It wasn't hours ago, it just feels like hours ago."

"Ro, it was hours ago." I ran my hand through my hair, blood throbbing hot in my ears. I was starting to think that was it, that we were gonna go the way of Hill and his sailors, that Ro had dragged us into the depths. There are stories of love-starved sailors out at sea too long, who look out at passing dolphins and see mermaids instead. I wondered if maybe it was the same with Ro's symbols. Maybe those trees we were following were actually blank, and we were only seeing the Xs because we wanted to see them.

Ro paused at the tree, staring out. Her face split into a grin as she pointed ahead. "Look the trees thin out ahead. I told you we were close. You panic too quickly."

"What you call panic, I call a healthy sense of self-preservation."

I looked up at the shreds of sky visible between the leaves, noticing how the pale blue was giving way to pink-stained clouds. The sun was sinking.

"Ah, you big baby," she laughed, more at ease now that the shore was in reach.

We hurried to the next tree, eyes trained on the X.

"As long as I'm an alive baby." I could see the trees thinning ahead, just as she'd said. But I couldn't smell the ocean. I couldn't hear the waves.

We got to the next carved tree. Past the trees was a clearing. No, clearing is too gentle a word. It was a crater.

Circled by jungle, the crater was at least half a mile wide. An empty blight of dead wood and smashed trees, haunted by the scent of smoke. No life. No sound. But I tell you, and I know how this sounds, but it's *true*, the earth was pulsing beneath my feet.

"How's this possible?" Ro breathed as we stepped in. "My marks ..."

"We must have passed by and not noticed." Ridiculous statement, but I wanted to sound sure because Ro didn't and one of us had to. I pushed aside some stray branches with my shoe, spotting streaks of ash. "Fire tore through here."

Ro let out a strangled laugh. "In a perfect circle?"

"Well, Christ, Ro, I don't know."

"Maybe it's in the journal," she said, taking it out from her waistband and opening it again. By now I wanted to cast the thing into the sea.

"I highly doubt that," I drawled, and looked out to the horizon. Trees, trees, and more trees. It went on forever.

Ro glared at me. "What do you know? Just about everything's in the journal."

And who knows? Maybe everything was. I never read the whole thing.

She stopped flipping through pages when she reached one in the center, shooting me a triumphant look. She turned the journal over to me to look at. I held it with just the tips of my fingers, as if the leather binding and yellowed pages were diseased. On the left page was a bird's eye sketch of a crater like this one, scattered with harsh pen strokes meant to imitate the fallen trees and debris, and eight crude human figures lingering at the edge of the jungle. Hanging above the sight was a blue smudge, labeled *The Light*. Written at the bottom was *'approximation of contact site based on the accounts of the* Mary Celeste*'s crew's first visit.'*

I didn't know about the *Mary Celeste* yet. It had set sail just a few months before we did, if memory serves. No one knew yet that in a few weeks' time it would drift to the coast of the Azores Islands, deserted.

Ro snatched the book back from me, eyes alight. "'Contact site'. Contact with what, do you think?"

"I'd rather not know." It came out harsh, but I was feeling harsh.

"The Way Crosser." Her eyes swept the page. "The Way Crosser, it was right here —"

"Ro, no."

"It's right here in the journal!" Ro looked up at the sky, which was growing darker by the moment. "This place is special, important. It's got the smell of transmutation, like Hill says."

"You don't even know what that word means," I scoffed.

"Change. Metamorphosis."

"We've gotta get back to the shore. To the ship." I shook my head and surveyed the ring in which we'd been caught. I had no clue how long we'd been gone. I wondered if they'd already sent a search party for us. A terrified part of me even wondered if they'd already set sail without us.

"If we stayed until it got dark, do you think we'd see the blue light?" Ro went on, still stuck in the world of the journal. "Do you think we'd find the Way Crosser?"

I grabbed her by the arm and tugged her back toward the trees. "We're going."

"No, wait —"

"Which of these is the tree you marked?" My eyes scanned the trees, locking on the first one I saw that bore the encircled X. But as I walked closer to it, I saw that the tree next to it was marked with the X, too. And the next one, and the next, and every tree all along the ring. Every single tree in sight was marked with the encircled X. It was as if Ro had marked the entire jungle.

The earth was thrumming with the air. The moon was crawling up past the treeline. In the space before a blink, I saw those eight figures, like they were standing with us in front of the trees. Waving. No, beckoning.

I couldn't bear to be there a single second more.

I ran right through the trees like mad. I didn't stop, I didn't look back, I didn't think. I just held on as tight to Ro as I could and ran and ran like fangs were snapping at my heels. I swear to God, something was breathing down my neck. Something was whispering at my back.

After what felt like an eternity, we tumbled past the trees. We looked down and beautifully familiar sand was under our feet. And not far off, there was our ship. There was our crew, scattered around the hull. Our Captain, directing them.

The Captain spotted us and jogged over. "Forgot something?"

I stared at him, blank-brained and goggle-eyed. "What?"

"You're back already." The Captain looked between me and Ro, confusion growing. "Why?"

"Already?" Ro blinked. "We were gone for hours."

"Hours? Ten minutes, maybe." He laughed, but not for long when he saw we weren't laughing with him.

I swallowed back bile. "I'm done. I'm going back to the ship."

I walked away from them both, not bothering to look behind as the Captain jeered.

"Christ, I hope you put in more of an effort if one of your own ever ends up lost."

•   •   •

By evening, we set sail, and there wasn't a soul on board happier than me. Ro and I didn't tell anyone about what we saw in the island's dark heart. I was ready to let it all fade, to dock in Hawaii and let everything go back to normal. The island, the ships, the journal, all could be forgotten. But there was Ro. She couldn't let it go.

The sun was setting the sky ablaze in red and pink. The ship was on the water. Oh, that gentle rise and fall with the water, it's like breathing. I was breathing again. Ro was right next to me, solid and real. Her eyes were on the island as we moved farther away.

She was beautiful. Sometimes it strikes me all at once, how beautiful she was. Her mind. Her spirit. Her laugh in the winds of a storm. I swear I hear it still when storms blow through.

She turned to me and asked, "What about the sailors?"

"We'll report it," I said, as if that would make a difference.

She looked back to the island. "What about the other things?"

I sighed and leaned on the railing, and gave what I thought was the best answer I could. "They don't matter now, Ro. They belong to the island. Just be with us and sail to Hawaii."

She didn't have anything to say to that. She could only keep watching the island. I really did want her to just be with us. With me.

For an hour, everything was okay.

For an hour, me, Ro, Jim, Mary, and Eddie all talked like normal, dwarfed by the stars above, eating and drinking a little. We were on shift for the next few hours. Ro was herself. And, you know, if it had just stayed clear that night, maybe this story would've ended better. If it had just stayed clear ... but then again, maybe not.

The storm struck us. We couldn't see our hands in front of us, and when the other crew members ran out with lanterns, that just made it worse. You could just see flashes of light, flashes of crewmates' faces, of their terror. Even Ro wasn't laughing at this one. Wind and rain battered us without mercy, lightning hit the water with a deafening crack, lighting the sky in blinding white. All I could taste was salt.

We were doing what we could. Striking the topmast. Tying ourselves to the ship with ropes, because if you went overboard in a storm the tides took you and that was that.

I looked around, stumbling. A flash of lantern light. Just enough for me to get a look at Ro a few feet away, just enough for me to see that the rope tied around her waist was fraying. It's something she would've normally noticed right away and jumped to fix. But she wasn't paying attention to the rope or the ship or my grabbing her shoulder.

"The light," she said, just loud enough to be heard above the storm. "The blue light!"

I pulled her closer, yelling into her ear. "Ro, your rope! It's gonna snap!"

"Do you see it?" She stared ahead.

"Just hang on to me, I'm gonna re-tie it." I took her rope in my hand, an unraveling tether holding her to the ship. I snapped the weak link, ready to knot it tighter. All she had to do was hold on to me. And she didn't even try.

Ro lunged forward, screaming about the light, a woman possessed. I had to wrap my arm around her waist and pin her to e just to keep her from sliding down the deck, my own rope pulled taut. She kicked at me, hit me, tried so hard to break free that two crewmates had to come and help me hold her. She fought us like it was for her life.

Mary's voice rang in my ear. "*What's wrong with her?*"

"*I don't know!*" It was all I could shout, over and over, and I couldn't tell if it was rain or tears streaming down my face.

The other crewmates held her against the mast and, God help me, I tied her to it so tight she could barely breathe. Still she flailed and squirmed against her bindings.

"The light! I see it! *Don't you see it?*"

None of us said anything to her as the storm tossed us. We were too terrified to speak. Not terrified of Ro going mad, though. We were terrified because we could see it too.

•　　•　　•

We survived the storm. And what a glorious release it was, when the clouds finally cleared, to not see a trace of that island.

It was morning by then. Ro hung limp against the ropes, passed out from having screamed herself hoarse through the night. The crew had all sorts of theories about her manic fit. Some rare tropical fever, Jim suggested. Dehydration, Eddie guessed. Overtired, too much sun, too little sun, food poisoning, everything you could think of other than the truth.

"Ro, I'm gonna untie you," I told her gently, waving a hand in front of her half-lidded eyes. "You got your wits back?"

She hesitated, then rasped, "Yes."

I undid the ropes slowly, my eyes continually flickering back to her, my guard up in case she went wild again. "It'll all be okay, Ro. It'll all be okay."

"Yeah, you're right," she said softly, flexing her hands as they were freed. "It will all be okay."

I stuck close to her the rest of the day. She didn't have any more mad fits, but she walked around in a daze. Her glassy eyes sought the horizon. I tried not to notice.

We just have to get to Hawaii, I kept thinking. *It'll be okay when we get to Hawaii.* She'll *be okay.*

We didn't quite know where we were, but the important thing was we were sailing away from the monster that had trapped us. I wouldn't have cared if we ended up in Shanghai, I just wanted to be somewhere I understood.

The hours were never longer. When the sun finally began to set, it felt like twenty years had passed rather than a day. I was supposed to take the first night shift with Ro. It would have been nice to sit with her and look at the stars. She knew the stories of all the constellations.

I leaned against the railing next to Ro as the others descended to their quarters below deck.

"Swear to Christ, there better not be another storm," I told her, watching the twilight sky for clouds.

She shook her head. "No. I think that was the last one."

"Good, good." I bit my lip. The island, everything we'd seen, hung heavy between us. I couldn't take it anymore. "Ro, last night —"

"Did you know Professor Hill brought a star map?" Ro cut me off. She was gazing out again, a ghost of a grin on her face.

I frowned. "What?"

Ro leaned closer to me, her shoulder pressed against mine. "A star map. It was buried at the bottom of his trunk. It goes with the other map we saw, the one with the blue lines. Pacifica."

"Pacifica," I echoed. The word sent the same shuddering in my bones that 'Way Crosser' did.

"That's why we couldn't make heads or tails of it. We're supposed to pair them together. Once I did that, the maps made complete sense."

I laughed uneasily, trying to sound more lighthearted than I felt. "Well, can they tell us how to get to Hawaii?"

"According to them, we're already on course."

"What?" I shot up straight, heart skipping a beat. "How do you know."

She gave me a strange look, then turned towards the sea and nodded. "Look down there."

I turned and looked. Dark waves rocked against the hull.

"What do you see?" Ro asked.

If I concentrated, I could just barely see it: the faint, glowing blue line beneath the ship. But I didn't want to see that. So I stopped concentrating, and the line I thought I saw faded until all that was left was the water that carried us.

"Nothing," I told her, pretending to myself that it was an honest answer. This expression passed over her face, something so sad and so full of longing. I blinked, and it was gone.

Ro stretched, yawned. "You hungry? I'm hungry."

"I could eat." I shrugged.

"Good, I've got some biscuits squirreled away in my quarters. They're the good ones, the ones Cap likes to hoard. I swiped them while he was busy earlier. You mind running and getting them from my quarters?"

"Sure," I said. I turned my back on her, went below deck, straight to her quarters. I looked around the room. I don't need to tell you there weren't any biscuits. What there was, was the journal propped up on her cot, with a folded note on the front.

READ ME

I should have run right back up the second I saw those words but, stupid, stupid me, I picked up the note, unfolded it, and read it through. The front of the note wasn't Ro's writing. It was what I guessed to be the last of Professor Hill's.

We are here. I am here, and, God, I am so afraid. It is terrifying when the choice is finally before you, yet exhilarating. So much possibility lies before me now. Soon we will know if all the stories are true, and see what so few of this world ever have. So many years in the dark, so many years studying, and now I find myself before the greatest of teachers. Monas was right. The secret is to let go so that you might be light enough to cross over. Let it all fall away. All along, the cure for pain was in the pain. I am unraveled. The light is brighter than ever. I am the Way Crosser.

It was a mad scrawl, as if he only had seconds to write it. Reading it made me reel, so I turned it over to be greeted by Ro's handwriting.

My dearest friend,

I find myself in a position that is difficult to describe. I think, for the first time, I am waking up from a dream. I need to know the truth. I need to know what Hill found. I need to cross the ways. I fear that if I don't, I will regret it all my life. I hope you and the others understand, and that you can forgive me. Wherever it is I'm going to now, I hope that someday, even if it takes a millennium, I see you there too.

Yours always,
Ro

I raced back above deck as fast as my legs could carry me, but it wasn't fast enough. A sweeping search of the ship only resulted in the realization that one of our rowboats was missing. So were the Pacifica map and the map of stars, I would later discover.

We begged the Captain to turn back for her. She was nowhere to be found on the open ocean and, after two days of circling the area, the Captain said we could delay no longer. We sailed to Hawaii, down one sailor.

I ransacked her quarters. I flipped that damn trunk upside-down, looking through clothes and tools and scholarly papers. None of it could tell me what I wanted to know. I ended up throwing myself on her cot, sobbing like a fool. She'd left the journal. I couldn't bring myself to read it, but I looked through some of Hill's sketches as I laid curled up on Ro's cot. Always, there was the blue light. Always, the memory of that light ignited a savage longing. When I looked up, the blue line was hanging above me, leading out the door to God knows where. *Follow me,* it seemed to pulse. I shut my eyes against it.

I dreamed of Ro every night since then. It's always the same dream. I'm always watching from the distance. She's in the boat, rowing toward the island, her strokes determined and sure. Ahead of her is the island, lit by a column of blue light shining from its center. The light is brighter than ever.

I came home to Washington. I got married, I had kids, I tried and mostly succeeded at living a quiet life. But that dream won't let me forget. You don't have to believe any of this, of course. You can chalk it all up to the ramblings of a crazy old sailor who's been in the bar too long, doesn't make a difference to me. I just figured at least someone else ought to know the whole story. I've never told anyone before you.

And now, someone will know where I went when I'm gone.

Look up, right above our heads. Do you see it? A blue line, bright as a beacon. I bet you see it, even if you won't admit it. It's been hanging over me lately. I think it's time I see where it leads.

ABOUT THE AUTHOR

Mia Ram is a fantasy and science-fiction writer from North Carolina. Her work has appeared in *Metaphorosis Magazine* and *The NoSleep Podcast*.

YOU MIGHT ALSO ENJOY

THE ALCHEMIST DAUGHTER
by Paul S. Moore

When a concoction of ethers channels a little of their magic properties to one location, inspiration springs to life.

GIFT OF SILENCE
by Alfred Smith

Mara's son is at the center of her burning city and his song out of control. She may not be able to save them both.

GREY MOTHER MOUNTAIN
by Elyse Russell

When her village is destroyed, an elderly woman seeks help from the last remaining dragon to get revenge.

Available in digital and trade paperback editions from
Water Dragon Publishing
waterdragonpublishing.com

www.ingramcontent.com/pod-product-compliance
Lightning Source LLC
Chambersburg PA
CBHW051303190726

48286CB00004B/1244